Vit Hopley is an artist ar
follows on from her firs
Wednesday Afternoon.

Blissful Islands is typeset in Libre Casion.

TO HELEN

The Copy Press Limited
51 South Street
Ventnor
Isle of Wight
PO38 1NG

copypress.co.uk

Commune no. 12
Editor: Kristen Kreider
Reader: Anne Tallentire
        Belinda Hopley
Copy-editor: Sara Peacock
Design: Opal Morgen/ John Peacock

Front cover © Vit Hopley

Printed on Munken Print White
no.18 80gsm. Munken Print White
standard products are FSCTM
and PEFC certified.

Printed and bound in England.

First edition © Copy Press Ltd/
Vit Hopley, 2018

Vit Hopley asserts the moral right
to be identified as the author of
this work.

A catalogue record for this book is
available from the British Library

ISBN-13   978-1-909570-05-4

BLISSFUL ISLANDS

Vit Hopley

· COPY PRESS

Contents

Eulogy

She who writes in blood and aphorisms does not want to be read, she wants to be learned by heart.

I expected to find her working at her desk. I found her in the bathroom brushing her teeth and combing her hair incessantly. She asked me to leave at once.

Contemporary

Railings, two gates, diagonal path, six benches, nine trees, shrubs: the square cuts a corner for her and allows pause for me. From opposite ends, within seconds of each other, we enter; I take a seat on the nearest bench as I always do and she, as she does, begins to walk across the square. Our movements coincide, since? since the first autumn leaf fell, exactly when I take my seat and she makes her way, her way? not my way, striding out, arms pulling forward, across the square, straight past me and through the gate without closing it behind her. This, this? keeps on happening; am I invisible to her? I should call out and say, say what? dare become that character who says it, out loud? to myself, crying out loud I am that whoever sitting here on a bench and she is walking towards me, past me and through the gate without closing it behind her. This keeps on happening. Of course she would not be there, there? looking back at me expressionless, unrecognisable, if it were not for me. I should make myself known immediately, immediately? when she has already left the square, and I have not yet decided whether to follow, follow? and close the gate behind me. From opposite ends, within seconds we enter; that we coincide with each other cannot to be left to chance.

Drawn Out

It is here, contained not confined, within this room that she will fulfil her potential. Four walls, ground and ceiling. Yellow walls, white ceiling. The floor is covered with pink carpet. In the middle of the floor there is a pillow; and a blanket, folded, green. When it is all too much she lies down. Sometimes she sits on the chair. Or she stands on the top rung of a five-step stepladder touching more than four walls. There is a wardrobe wedged into the left-hand alcove farthest from the window.

The description of this room lacks measure: a gentle six paces wide and eight long and, although situated at the top of the house, it is not in the eaves; let the ladder suggest its height. She can almost hear herself rattle though speculation might say that if she were to share this room with more things it would not be so. Just yesterday, whilst cleaning a few cobwebs from the top of the window, she discovered a palm's worth of uninterrupted view between the rooftops of the neighbouring houses. She immediately imagined the possibility of this small space being filled with blinding sunlight. Ludicrous. And even more so that she would be standing on that ladder, there, at the precise time when it might happen. The ladder has not been moved.

Close by, on the floor, near the chair, lies the smallest of mirrors, a pocket mirror. She can and she does occasionally look down into it. An eye, sagging flesh, wrinkled, cracked lip, parts here and there, never the whole—too much to bear—skin separating from skeleton is a terrifying sight, and a stark reminder that it may be true that it is only the young who qualify looking down on the world. There is not a table in this room; she makes do with the floor or her lap.

It is quiet. How often does such silence occur without being imbued with foreboding? Those truly peaceful days when the world lays itself bare, time stretches aimlessly; it is as though she is floating. Yet it changes all too suddenly. A simple thought in the wrong direction, a noise, a whatever, and she is swimming for her life. Why? It must stem from a quandary between giving and receiving. Take this chair. She can neither sit upright nor slump with ease. Is it the nature of the chair or the fact that she has short legs and a long body? What gives in this situation cannot totally be received, let alone grasped, and that is keeping her on her feet.

She is pacing. Heard from below, pacing is indicative of someone involved in a heated discussion or waiting impatiently. She is doing neither. She is just pacing. She hasn't received a visitor in this room for weeks. She is not expecting one today nor in the near future, but she does fear one who might bring deliverance concealed in friendship. Visitors such as these have absolute faith that their presence and a few simple words are enough to open the way. Slate clean, begin anew. How could she resist? She is pacing.

She is without electric light. It is a simple enough task to change a light bulb but she has not. The day tells her when it is over. The afternoon light rakes in, highlighting a spoon left on the windowsill. When the first ant arrived she was surprised but not at all by the others that followed. How astonishing it is that these small beasts climb such heights. Predictable and uniform; tedium must drive them forward. She dipped the spoon in honey: a small sun in itself. It took less than a day for the ants to create a partial eclipse. They will never leave.

It was a real discovery to find a pile of paper stored at the back of the wardrobe. It had been there all the time and long enough to collect a fine layer of dust. She has carefully wiped the dust off and counted every sheet. A single ream of plain white paper. There is beauty to be found in the knowledge that something is complete. If she was to remove one sheet of paper it could become everyday and paper is nothing everyday, yet what can she do with so much paper? Eventually dust will separate the sheets.

For the love of the diagram and labour involved she has pinned a family tree to the wall. The document, sent by a distant relative, so distant she was unaware of their existence, is the size of a poster. Spanning at least seven generations, there are over 100 names. The thought of the potential information contained within each name is overwhelming. Her name connects above, but off centre, to the next generation and within one generation she is amongst strangers. The bottom right corner of the document is curling where one drawing pin is missing. The pin has fallen pinpoint up and is obscured by the pile of the carpet.

She is pacing. Seen from above pacing is indicative of someone deep in thought or profoundly bored. She is neither. She is just stretching her legs. There is nothing on her mind though she does fear thoughts that contain only a remembering of injustice and regret. Such thoughts have a habit of rising up from underneath; the past is dragged backwards awakening pain long buried, only to deny the truth of the very emotion itself. What a life. There is no future in remembering like this; she prefers to forget. She is pacing.

She is so utterly unremarkable that she cannot ignore who she is, but the mystery that surrounds her is not recognisable. A rope dangling from the middle of the ceiling, a knife placed in her hand or any such object could assist in locating her significance. She is holding a walnut in the palm of her hand; pulling in opposite directions her lips, stretching over her teeth, smile, her mouth opens, laugh. It is a difficult task to keep such a life alive, yet to laugh is to risk all that is known and loved, for laughter draws on the out breath of death.

She is laughing.

Witness

There was no reason for her to get up but she did. Once up, she decided that she had grown tired of looking at the shadowy backs of the five ornamental cats sitting on the windowsill, behind the net curtain. Each one was lovingly turned to face inward. She left the net curtain drawn open and returned to her chair. The thick layer of dust covering the cats and the windowsill did not concern her.

Five friendly faces all in a line taking her back. She fixed her gaze past the cats, straight through the concerned face pressed up against the window, and beyond. She heard the tap at the window, she heard the dog bark, she knew it was the woman who lived four doors away. Then, coming through the letterbox, barely audible amongst the woofs and yaps, she heard her name being called. There was no reason for her to get up; why move or even blink for that matter? She does admire dogs but never enough not to say she prefers cats.

There was no reason for her to get up but she did. Once up, she decided the room had become a little too bright. She lovingly turned each cat to face outward, drew the net curtain, and returned to her chair.

Providence

During a weary moment between chapters of a weary book, he found himself distracted by the weight of his head. He got up from his desk. It did not occur to him to open a window, read a different book or sit on a more comfortable chair. Instead he went into his bathroom and stood in front of the mirror. What he saw was a large head resting on too thin a neck; a puny column, terrifyingly fragile, overburdened.

It took five days for the neck brace to arrive, during which time, tormented by thoughts of what might happen, he kept his head as still as possible.

The brace fitted perfectly and although it restricted his movement considerably he was happy, almost light headed. It did not occur to him to consider the potential dangers that he would now, quite literally, be unable to face. This may be why he disregarded the three people standing in front of him, gesturing and pointing in an upward direction.

The first brick that fell from the pile of falling bricks landed on his head and killed him outright.

Epiphany

The bus is running on time. She had not seen the
rain coming. Clearly. She is not the only one to be
caught. The bus windows are steamed up. She does
not complain. Someone younger in years offers their
seat. She sits down, places her briefcase on her lap
and begins to wipe dry the raindrops with her sleeve.
A person recognises her as the spiritual healer; the
spiritual healer avoids eye contact. That person,
she remembers, substituted loneliness with a slight
limp; the gift was no more use to them than to the
bad-tempered cat who had not taken kindly to the
laying-on of hands. The gift, passed down to her
through generations: down to her, she wonders—
does she really have the gift? Epiphany, blinding
revelation, the sun emerges catching every raindrop
as it appears; the bus swerves off the road into a ditch.

Because I Can

I am standing at my window, positioned perfectly, three floors up, overlooking the street. My street, the street I live on, is like so many others: post delivered, milk delivered, screaming children late for school, dogs walked, cars on their way; always extraordinary and, observing from above, nothing goes unnoticed. Today: a walking stick, two bags, a vital headscarf, a coat missing all but one button, and a fallen handkerchief. Two bags and her knees not bending hinder pick-up. Don't stop; move on.

This is neither the time nor the place to linger. The wind is picking up.

Hesitating, struggling, fussing, bundled. Her walking stick is hooked on the coat button. One bag hangs on her wrist and the other is open. A bag inside the bag is taken out. Three bags. Now two bags are hanging on her wrist; the other is open. A clean handkerchief is taken out and stuffed in a pocket. Bag shut. Headscarf flapping, about to fly; free hand on head. Lopsided.

Narrow streets lined with terraced houses act as wind tunnels. A single gust and she will be felled.

Bags down. She moves to a low wall and sits. A forgotten walking stick becomes a nuisance, yet with two free hands she secures her headscarf and proceeds to empty one bag into one and place it in the other. One big bag. Her headscarf is tied firmly with a double knot, but she is without gloves. Must be an oversight. Exposed.

She can't sit there all day. The wind whips round that bend in the street.

Up. Weighed down. She takes a few steps here, a few steps there. Round the bend, down the alley, into the yard. Forward and back. Round the bend, down the alley, into the yard. Confused? Wind blows off balance. She looks down. Her walking stick has fallen. Big bag pulling on one hand, and handkerchief in the other: both hands are full. She looks up. Rain clouds are collecting.

Poised. I can't wait for what happens next. I must intervene. Without hesitation I take three flights of stairs, two steps at a time, open the door, step outside, and the door shuts. All in a flash. Where is she? I take a few steps here, a few steps there. Forward and back. Gone. Round the bend, down the alley, into the yard. Disappeared. She is nowhere to be seen. I take a seat on the low wall. No hat, no coat, no scarf, no keys. A car draws up. There, sheltered from behind a high wall, walking stick first, she appears. One big bag is now two bags again. She has a rain hat on; her headscarf makes a pretty cravat. The car door is opened. Bag then bag, walking stick next, a helping hand, all in. Door shut and away.

Locked out. Wind and rain are a dreadful combination.

Custodian

The dead bird was placed on a sheet of newspaper for me to see. I did not want to look. I imagined seeing more than just a dead bird. I did look. A single white feather, the only discernable feather, caught my eye and nothing else. It was not as easy to remove as I expected.

This house has belonged to my family for well over 100 years and its chimneys have always been swept on 12th March. The reason for this date and no other has been lost over the years and, even though the fires are no longer lit and central heating has been installed, I have carried on the tradition. Since the discovery of the dead bird in one of the chimneys I have decided to board up all the fireplaces.

The piece of broken pottery that I had found looked interesting in the hands of the local historian. In his delicate hand, subject to the manner in which he conducted his interrogations, the fragment was saying all it could say. My imagination ran wild. He returned the piece to me without saying a word. A couple of days later I was struck by the disappointment that he had not worn white gloves.

The museum receptionist and I depend upon one another. She provides the welcome and I the security. She holds the keys and prepares the museum for opening, but it is not until I arrive that the closed sign is turned to open. The anomaly here is not eased by her insistence that a closed sign is as good as a lock.

The piece of broken pottery and feather on the mantelpiece are not considered to be souvenirs, as that would reduce their potential significance enormously. Equally, any attempt to seek a connection between the two bears only the obvious. I am free to throw a multitude of questions at them, just as they are.

If the chance had arisen I would have argued strongly against those who deemed it unnecessary to dress the museum guard in uniform. Suffice to say, I have perfected my demeanour such that I need only fall back on myself.

I am waiting for the opportunity to arise when I might suggest to the receptionist that she consider refreshing the flowers or removing the heater from under her desk. I suspect another winter may pass.

When the strong north-easterly winds blow, I would find myself peering up inside the chimney. The only flapping wings to be seen were created by my torchlight.

A cup, a pen, a something, on one occasion half a biscuit; the historian always says in one way or another that he has been in. It is up to me to notice the changes that have taken place. I haven't been sleeping at all well since the dead bird was found.

The museum can be so quiet; the stillness of the exhibits speaks such that even the dust refuses to settle. Being the last of a long family line carries no more or less of a burden than any of these exhibits I watch over. What will follow?

Being a presence felt without creating a distraction requires absolute focus. It was recently suggested that during quiet periods I should take a rest and read a book, but I prefer, when no one is looking, to clear the museum of its dead flies. Rarely do I see one buzzing around, so it is quite bizarre that I find three or four dead daily.

Once, and it has not happened since, a visitor I suspected to be drunk who was in fact bewildered insisted on trying to exit the museum through a locked door labelled PRIVATE NO ENTRY. No matter how hard I tried I was unable to convince him that he had entered the museum through an open door.

There are days when I see myself before every exhibit. Reflecting.

A Blessing

She put her head into her hands and said—listen to me listen to me—she put her hands onto her head and she said—listen to me listen to me—it is no good, there is no good.

Nostalgia

I have no desire to introduce myself; you might think
that this suggests a rather unwilling character, but
you would be mistaken. All you need to know is that I
have been away and have just returned home. I notice
the word 'just'. To be precise, one week ago I set out
my return: planning a night hour so as to encounter
no one, I was to slide back home, not creep but slide
without interruption; how I wished to go unnoticed.
In retrospect I realise that this was a foolish desire;
my plan was flawed. Why? Realistically, the last train
never arrives late enough and during those spare
hours, barely past dark, loitering, I would not fail to
be noticed. And let's not forget there is always a dog
waiting to bark, door hinges needing oil, floorboards
that creak and, in the dark of night, to trip, bump or
knock is commonplace. It was just past midnight when
I walked through the front door. My aunt, holding a
stick in one hand and an empty glass vase in the other,
was waiting to greet me.

   —It's me. For then she decided to show pleasure;
it was the following day that I was to receive her true
disappointment. What did I expect? Creeping in, after
not even a word, with nothing to say for myself. To
come and go without demand? Yes. Clearly she had
suffered a range of emotion and I, with such ease, have
created the impression of a thoughtless character. Yet I
assure you my actions have not been without thought.
—It's me. An inadequate explanation. My aunt. Silent.
Is she best described by the small cowbell hanging
on the garden gate, the house, its furniture, polished

stairs, curtains, a bottom drawer or the small hole in
her cardigan that's not saying anything, watery eyes,
short grey hair, which she cuts and styles herself?
She is holding a mug, chipped, in her left hand, her
fingernail is chipped, all things chipped, ornaments
chip, she has a chipped upper left lateral incisor.
Yawning. Yellow old teeth. Are you tired? She lost the
other by accident, the lower right third molar left of
its own accord, more will follow, but in the meantime
there is nothing to chew on here, only questions
exhausted in my absence. —It's me. The cat, not quite
ready to shake off the cat she is to be our cat, saunters
in, muddy paws still prowling. Little black and white
twice-fed butterball cat whose delicate nails, so
razor sharp, can easily turn a rabbit inside out, where
have you been? Here, there, never far away, jump up
pussycat, pussycat; I think if there is to be any realism
here: the cat being a cat is ignoring me. —It's only
me. Can be no other than the neighbour who only
ever enters via the back door though rarely crosses
the threshold; she is not stopping, just passing, and
won't come in; dirty boots, must walk the dog, must
not be late, parish council meeting, village dustbins
to discuss, a new terrorist threat or was that global
warming, anyway; she heard a kerfuffle last night,
suffered a sleepless night, and is just checking there
is nothing to report. Just (that word again), just the
passivity of semi-detached living: oh it's you.

   —It's you. You there and she there, exactly, you
and your aunt are sitting either side of the kitchen

table, this is quite usual, you know your place and she knows hers. This seating arrangement, without fail, returns you to you, memories hoard in, they can't wait to be recalled, (surely they don't have a will of their own); back you go, to where, this time, really that far back. OK. And you wonder where all the time goes. Sitting. You have in front of you, in your possession, a scrap of paper, folded, probably a back of an envelope, unfolded, a list, that you refold only to unfold to refold, folding an infinite increase in the number of creases the paper can hold; the cat's kneading paws and purrs are doing the work of the domesticated. Hold still this image in your mind. The neighbour is poking her head around the door; both you and your aunt have turned to look at her. She, that is the neighbour, is saying one more thing and (that's another thing too) then she really must go. Yes, yes it is spring; the door has been kept open for more than ten minutes, she is not coming in but air enlivened by a higher sun is: filling air space.

It is spring. The glass vase has been filled with daffodils. Early this morning you saw your aunt in the garden move from daffodil clump to daffodil clump; she was being careful to take only those flowers that would not be missed. Daffodils: the chaplet of infernal gods. Narcissi: benumbing youth. Stop there. While you might vainly read too much into these daffodils the expression on your aunt's face is unchanging. Puckered brow, pursed lips. Is she troubling a thought, a thought that escapes her, that will, when she least expects, return to her? She is not one to dwell, her mind is blank. Filling air space. Stop there. The neighbour was saying one more thing, and the cat, oblivious or not, has wandered off. Daffodils. Daffodils again, forgive me.

Forgive me. Me. I cannot explain my significance any more than you or she can; setting out is hard enough. —It's me. The interruption I fear. —It's only me. The neighbour. Still here. Is she best described by her dogged commitment to the community or by her ability to become as intrusive as a bad memory; and just one more thing (and I will close the door behind me), will she ever leave? —It's me. A cat, not our cat, slinks in; mangy old curious cat, gnawed ear, kinked-tail cat you don't belong here! Shoo pussycat shoo out you go before our cat comes back and my aunt takes her stick to you. The neighbour is poking her head around the door and my aunt is looking away. What are you waiting for; the day is moving on. The cat not our cat has left exactly as it came in, through the open door—ah, the audacity—the neighbour left without closing the door behind her and, just (not that word again) as I am about to close the door, my aunt, having waited all this time, desperate to say something, asks —Are you staying? You close the door behind you.

Forsake

Tongues, drawl, tails and wet paws. And dogs tugging at leads. Her wrist is chafed raw. Damp, cold, metallic tasting; morning dew. And the smell of cracked paving. Her foot slightly twists as she falls. Barking, barking mad; down she goes, grazing her knee and cracking her head; nothing can break her fall. And the neighbours watch.

Get up, get up, for god's sake get up: tongues are wagging.

Tongue: bare word spoken noisily with the mouth. And wind, shadow, storm and sorrow speak incessantly. In tongues: babbling, twittering, chattering, whispering the most ancient and holy of languages that to our ears is more than the heart can think. Confounded. Me: simple word pawing and licking, sweet and delectable; and I, falling and rising, caught between heaven and earth like a dog's howl, unable to speak for myself. Maddening. Her foot is not wholly in her shoe. And her shoe is not wholly on her foot.

Someone calls the doctor, someone calls the priest; and everyone calls each other. No one calls her; she is presumed dead.

Blind Faith

Stone cottages, powdery stones, perforated mortar, nooks for minuscule creatures, rusty hooks, falling climbing vegetation, cobwebs shroud flaking paint; windows are small, dark and hard to look through; inside the sills are wide. The garden is walled. The wall is made with local stone: the stone, a warm glittering mix of sand and shells. Sitting on the wall in a rusty biscuit tin there is a jam jar with fifty pence in it and a stone weighing down a piece of paper with fifty pence written on it. The garden gate: odd bits of wood pieced together, a streak of red paint and the word GEESE.

She is walking up the garden path; a goose follows and two more appear from amongst the high weeds of a once made garden. Salutations, all bustle, hands and cloth, beckoning and urgent: I know to wait. She opens the gate: I know to walk in front. Heading the train down the garden path: I know to keep her between her geese and me. —Hush that hissing behind my back: I know to keep to the path.

The door to the cottage opens straight into the kitchen, a kitchen more outside than in: the table, a no particular place, is piled high with anything; the shelves are too. The floor is cold and muddy; slug trails pattern the walls. Behind the kitchen sink, jars with cuttings at various stages of rooting and rotting clutter the sill; and in the sink the washing-up is waiting another day. A bucket of water with two leaves floating on top and an old rag beside it lie interrupted. There is only one chair and on it there is an old alarm clock, wind-up with bells, and a tray laid for tea for one.

She lives alone with her mother. She has always cared for her dear old mother, it has always been so; and I ask, was her mother always old and dear?

A sliding door leads into a hallway: a picture askew, a vase with no flowers, a coat rack with no coats, a clock; whose decision was it to seal the front entrance to this cottage. A large mirror, which fills a wall and does no more than that, hangs above and over a table; on the table dust and dead—four flies, a couple of moths and a beetle—have been swept into a tidy mound and left. This is a dismal space to pass through however quickly.

She is close behind, ushering me forwards like one of her geese; if she had a stick she would use it, if I could move faster I would. I have my coat hanging over my arm: I know not to stay too long. And a pot of jam in my hand: I know the dear, old mother tires. The jam is for her: I know to leave before the alarm clock rings for tea.

I am taken into a darkened room: the curtains are drawn, subdued light emanates from a table lamp and a vague glow from a three-bar gas fire; my eyes stretch wide to adjust. In a shadowy recess there is a desk clear of objects; a bookshelf fills one wall, indefinite pictures decorate the others. Her mother is sitting in an armchair; there is a footstool and a small low table beside her. There is an absence of any other chairs.

A frail arm reaches out, gesturing for me to come closer. She is virtually blind: I know to stand in the light of the fire. Her eyes remain open, unable to close even in sleep; she sees everything: I know sight is too much for her to bear. Withdrawn to this room she lives in the darkness of the heavens: I know not to ask questions; they dissolve in her.

Her body is appallingly old; cradled in the armchair, parched and brittle on the brink of ruin, her collapsed features express life in its entirety, and her eyes, piercing black holes, a spirited darkness. She is present. And I begin speaking as though time were running out yet with a voice arrestingly loud: my mouth, gaping black hole, spewing word after word as if volume will produce proximity—dear old mother I am here—dropped like a stone into a well—dear old mother are you there—absorbed in a depth of darkness—dear old mother where are you—incessant and forgetful as the spring its source—dear old mother are you here—babbling on without end.

The warm dark air of the room stifles a yawn; the backs of my legs burn from standing too close to the fire; her head nods forward. All too quickly. There is no time for farewells; I am ushered from the room, through the dingy hall, into the kitchen and out into the bright light of the day. My wide-open eyes strive to see. Blinding pools of black light dissolve into a rapid flux of light and shadow: a flurry of wings, phantoms, angelic hosts or attacking geese chasing me up the garden path.

In the distance, behind me, the alarm clock rings.

Wisdom

A picture.

A child is held tight, restrained—that's dramatic.
A child is held tight, loosely shackled—still dramatic.
A child is held tight within her arms. Her, that is my
mother. I am held tight within my mother's arms.
Look, everyone is looking. Everyone, that is my family,
looking towards a camera. Five forthright faces look
directly; as for the other 26 faces negligible distractions
skew the ideal, yet they are all smiling for the moment.
And me—ah yes—there I am, held tight in my
mother's arms, hair in disarray, contorted. I, apple of
my mother's eye, wriggling like a maggot in windfall.

A maggot, the smallest of serpents. Poor old
serpent: Adam blamed Eve and Eve blamed you and
who can I blame?

Making history.

Two women are sitting side by side at a kitchen
table with their backs against the warmth of a stove.
One near blind, eye bags sodden, trembles all over,
and the other a frail shell lost amongst a sack of loose
skin. On the brink. The room is dark. The room
smells. Stone floors, rotting apples. The kitchen
table, dark oak. Opposite, held against the warmth
of my mother, I am wriggling like a maggot in
windfall. My mother speaks very loudly. She says
—Hold still. She says —Behave. She says —When
will you learn. She says all this and proclaims even
more on my behalf. Across the kitchen table.

The distance between us is vast. In the middle of

the table there stands a solitary glass of apple juice, cloudy with sediment slowly sinking. It is waiting for me. It always is. And as always, before coming here, my mother has said, as her mother said to her and her mother's mother said to her —There will be no argument, when the juice clears you must drink, not before, and only then may you go out to play. Sour apples. A lesson in patience sinking in: apples from trees generations-old pressed dry, what does that tell me? A lesson in trust sinking in: apples from trees generations-old pressed dry, what does that show me?

My mother, insistent that I have a question to ask, tightens her grip and tips me forward—rattled, tongue rolling in an empty mouth, not word nor sound will be found in me—and over my head she asks after the trees; she asks after the apples; she asks after the sweetness of juice; she asks the same questions every time and more on my behalf. Opposite, the women speak; words rise deep from the belly only to be caught at the back of the throat; guttural babbling swallows them up while mother's tongue acts quickly to salvage anything it can.

So here we all are. Again.

My mother speaks of harsh winters past, violent storms, trees falling, her mother their mothers, apple canker, my school report, the roof, a hip, a knee, nothing short of a miracle, the doctor and two doors down. —Hold still. The old garden wall, wasps, maggoty apples. —Behave. Sunlight from the garden is caught amongst leaves of geranium plants sitting on the windowsill; sporadic rays streak brilliance across the dim light of the room. How much longer must I wait? Opposite, in amongst the wrinkles, old and wise, a lifetime squeezed dry touches eternity. —When will you learn.

Sediment falling.

For as long as it has taken and my mother's grip loosens enough for me to fall freely out of her arms, in no time the juice is drunk, and in no time she is calling after me. —Not yet. And I am already half way up the garden path. —Wait. Running towards the old orchard. —Careful. Don't the first moments of independence come with limitless freedom. A pile of rubble is all that remains of the garden wall and, within, a dozen apple trees, knee-high weeds, nettles and thistles; an upturned chair and bucket beside a knife stabbed into earth; another chair under a tree, a wooden ladder propped against a trunk and knotted rope hangs from an old metal climbing frame.

Sharp afternoon shadows fall.

I am absolutely alone. Here, a wasteland. Every sound, every shape a noisy play of light and shadow. Dewdrops glisten, leaves flutter, ground squelches. Swinging from the top bar of the climbing frame, cold metal grips my skeleton. Letting go, thistles prick through my socks. Moving between trees, jumping shadows; tripping over a stone, whatever lives underneath will have the world as they find it. I have found the knife and I am using it to flick open moss-filled cracks. This is it. Looking over my own shoulder

I am an archaeologist, a pioneer who finds no shame in not knowing everything in the world as if from birth. In this dilapidated orchard, behind my back the sun is setting.

In no time, I am being called.

Grace

—Living the day is giving back what belongs to the night.

If Grandmother said it once, she said it again. The second saying in her mind exhausted the banality of what was being said and was more desirable than a sigh.

—Living the day is giving back what belongs to the night.

My grandmother. Her bedroom: light and spacious. Her dressing table: cluttered. Me: standing perfectly still but for a finger running a line through powder. I am to stand just there and not there since if she wanted shadows dancing all over her she might as well have a vase of cut flowers on the windowsill. Cut flowers are for funerals, potpourri for the dead, and never make a gift of anything other than a living plant. Empty windowsills and my grandmother putting her face on. The dressing table mirror is angled just so, tilted upwards to catch her in the best light, and jammed in place with a jet-stone rosary coiled around its loose hinges. The little black beads belong there, after all, at the end of the day, when all is said and done too much time is spent counting and not enough time looking in the mirror.

Facing herself, she rubs her face; a little blood rising in the cheeks and a dab of powder brings any face out of the wilderness. Powdery haze. Here I am. Radiant, shining with bright rays, there is no time like the present and what can we do with that, she says. Heaven on earth, we must not be late, he is waiting for us.

Us: Grandmother, dog, basket and me all gathered together in the car, windows wide open, panting frosty breath. He: the old man stands at the window looking out onto his garden path. He leans on the windowsill, waits, and when we do not arrive he disappears; his breath leaves a ghostly patch. A few moments later he returns: his face emerges from darkness, and when we do not arrive he disappears again: shadowy blur, toing and froing, toing and froing. His face at the window. The garden path, a straight line running through rough grass, leading to his door. We arrive. Yoo-hoo hello rattles through the letterbox, the dog comes and goes, and the old man dodders; in his time he opens the door.

There is no light. The hallway is dark, grey like the bare floors and his battered old suit; in the front room an empty light socket dangles in the middle of the ceiling. On the small table is a mug and a plate resting on a sheet of newspaper. There is only one chair. Grandmother holds the back of it while he leans on the table. I am standing there, just there, beside the fireplace. On the mantelpiece there is a travel clock and a postcard of an isolated mountain. And nothing else.

He is deaf and she is asking this and that. Bellowed words fill the room like day encounters night; in time, a short time, words mumble and lapse. Nodding. There is enough understanding between them to mute language. Silence amplifies a wagging tail; I shift my weight from one foot to the other. Sunlight pushes shadows of broken cloud flickering across the back wall, dust poised in its rays. A silent, moving image.

Highlights and halos, there is no time like the present, faces open for what is to come, eyes share a glint. Here we all are, done with words; and the dog is restless.

Grace is an unanswered prayer.

Crane Fly

Come back. Her refusal of this command placed her firmly in a world of past and future. There was no going back; for the first time in her life she had direction, she was looking forward; she was in search of happiness. Where better to find it than amongst autumn leaves, where better than in spring buds, where better than in dappled summer sunlight, where better than in a winter haw frost. Come back. Where better than in this instance of refusal. In a moment that pays heed to a history that repeats itself, she has found eternal happiness. Dizzy. Barefoot, ankle deep, she squeezes decaying leaves between her toes as autumn colour rustles around her. Come back. A line must be drawn here lest her legs buckle and she meets her descent albeit with the grace of the crane fly, whose long limbs fold to create the frame that keeps its body held above ground, suspended, for eternity.

Meteor

What I cannot account for: the speed of gathering speed, shooting through air, the thrill.

What I cannot account for: the moment running away with itself, excitement and anticipation tighten, the resistance in stopping.

Beyond where I can see you, in earshot and not too far, around the corner, up the hill and down, there I am.

At a stop.

A bicycle is lying in the road, the back wheel is still spinning; it stopped abruptly when it hit a grassy verge and I, catapulted over the handlebars, landed in a ditch.

Cloud, sky, cloud, low sunlight flitting amongst drops of dew, and wind enough for rooks to take to the sky. The ditch is clogged with rotten leaves, grasses, nettles, bramble. Caught. The smell of mud and fields. In the ditch sound trickles, scrapes, whispers. Here my breath is hollow.

What just happened?

A spectacular event, a spectacular fall and there is not a soul in sight. Nothing remains, not even the cry that followed me down the hill; it is as if I have come from nowhere.

Dampness seeps, movement entangled; jabs, stings and bites; coiling and pressing, cold bores. Ditch life. The hedge sings, leaves flutter. Turning inward I echo inside: when a rock falls from high in the sky there is a flash, a spark, a streak of light; burning into the earth's atmosphere nothing survives its journey.

Do I wish come and find me.

I close my eyes, shadows flock to aberrant light.

Caravan

High hedges, narrow roads bend, there in that small clearing on the corner a caravan has been parked for longer than anyone can remember. How it got there, who put it there, no one knows. It grows out of the hedge covered in moss; two small windows look out and as each day ends a light burns into the night. The caravan belongs to the corner, it belongs to the hedge, it belongs to the night sky.

He lives in the caravan and has done so for as long as anyone can remember. When he arrived no one knows. The anyones and no ones would prefer the caravan was not there. They say in strong words it is a hazard, a danger. They want to say he should move on. What can they do? The land in the corner belongs to no one anyone knows, who probably owns the caravan too.

They belong to the village and the village is a mile down the road. A mile down the road is a short drive. A mile down the road is a short walk on the road. He walks, they pass quickly in their cars. Even when it is raining. You see, the sun shines; they pass quickly, he blurs into the hedge, a smudge. Every day. He walks into the village, past her house.

Her house, a white stone house with four windows and a front door; the village, settled in a hollow, has a single road running through. The house is in the middle of the village. Once it belonged to the farm but the road separated the farm from the house and the house from the farm. Now the house belongs to her and it is close to the road; nothing passes without rattling the windows.

She stares from the kitchen window. Every day, looking at nothing in particular, thinking nothing in particular; at a standstill, her silence unfurls air without a word to wrap itself around. You see, she is alone watching a world go by. It all happens out there and stays out there. They say she should not live on her own. They say she is isolated. Days pass quickly. Every day waiting, waiting for another day.

On this day the skies have opened. There he is, bowed, caught without cover, his hands making a small shelter above his head, heavy drops splashing back high. There she is muttering, caught by surprise; rain hits hard against the window, mouthed words fall to the ground. Continual rain. Rivulets run down the road, streaming across the window, her hand involuntarily wipes aside, demystifying the view; he walks on water.

And on this day, she sees something, something that takes her away from the window towards the front door. She grabs an umbrella, steps outside into the pouring rain, and sets off in his direction. He has passed her house and is already half way up the hill towards the village shop. Drenched. She runs, runs up the hill gesturing —You —You, the umbrella points.

There they are, at the top of the hill, under the shelter of the umbrella, in a circle of spray. She and he, face to face. You see, they are looking at each other; eyes wide open, she falls into black holes and he too, deeper than he can go. Yet, with nothing between them, they share an unthinkable closeness only to be repelled by their own reflections. She sees herself, he sees himself. You see, a small break in the cloud momentarily caught in drops of rain glistens.

Glistening. A split second, caught in the glint of an eye, a fathomless puddle. Now he is holding the umbrella and she is walking down the hill towards home; she uses her free hands to make a small shelter above her head. Light dances in rain, clouds slip from shining puddles, black holes open. You see, grasping this moment makes your eyes water, takes you back.

She is looking out of her kitchen window. It has stopped raining. There he is, walking by, a bottle of milk in one hand and nothing in the other. The umbrella has been forgotten, left behind on the step of the shop, dripping. He might remember tomorrow. The skies open. Afternoon light, full of flare, streams through her window; her hand instinctively rises to shield her eyes; he is bathed in light. Blinding. Time passes quickly.

And this day ends, every day a procession of time; the setting sun drops out of sight, darkness sits in the hollow, the house disappears but for a thin line of light shining through the split between the curtains. You see, the day returns to the night, it belongs to the night, it belongs to the night sky.

Peninsula

The back door of the house has been left open.

It was someone's good decision to build here and to build this house in particular. The house changed hands, each time returning it to its beginning; eventually, for what now seems a lifetime ago, the house was passed to me. All of a sudden I am not so young any more.

Stone steps, dirt-filled cracks alive; timber-framed weatherboard house in its element. Inside. A house occupied with history. Old rug, coat pegs without coats, a boot; objects and photographs, keepsakes of memory that has vanished. Something began here, yet infinitely distances itself.

Three picture windows look out onto the lake. The lake, a mirroring surface for light and wind; red setting and rising, radiant pools, shadow laps the water's edge. All around, trees. Light from secluded dwellings draws the night down over the lake. Starry night. One by one the lights go out.

There is a flagpole beside the house; redundant, the cord thrums against the pole. Raise the flag: someone has arrived, is belonging, has died, is still here, I surrender our collective solitude. Conventions, like people, drop away. One day I woke up alone.

A path begins at the back of the house, drops straight down to follow the edge of the lake, then narrows, winding through birch and pine to open onto a stretch of gravelly stone and boulders. The beach. It is out of the way; I am here.

Naked, knee deep in water, my reflection shrouded,

I plunge. Cold water grips, warm blood rushes: I give up, I give in. The lake. Inside, remoteness surrounds me; below the surface, in darkness, solitude is without memory or beginning.

The outside light of the house has been left on.

Landscape

She is leaning against a tree, she is lying in grass, she is sitting on a rock. In a graveyard. The tree is oak, the grass rough, the rock juts out. Birdsong.

She held me in her arms until I was out of reach. She lay in my arms until she died. Hold me so I might remember.

She told me what she knew until I made no sense. She kept all my secrets until she died. Say something so I might remember.

She sang me songs until I vanished. She heard my song until she died. Sing so I might remember.

A tree touched by wind stretches its roots wide. The ground gives way to what is coming. A rock, buoyed in earth, heaves.

I keep returning—she wraps her arms around the tree—touching what has vanished.

Am I close—she presses her ear to the ground—inaudible words hiss in my ear.

Closer to the truth—she places her head in her hands—shaping memory in forgetting.

A bird, somewhere, out of sight, perches on a branch; the tree sings its song, a phrase here and there. The grass quivers. The rock glints sunlight.

I wonder—she walks around the tree—without her where would I be.

I am listening—she rolls over on the ground—where would I put my attention.

I remember—she looks up to the sky—my precarious attitude.

Future Editions

For future editions, please visit the Copy Press website

Copy Press is committed to bringing readers and writers together and invites you to join its Reader's Union – please visit www.copypress.co.uk